Honeypot Hill

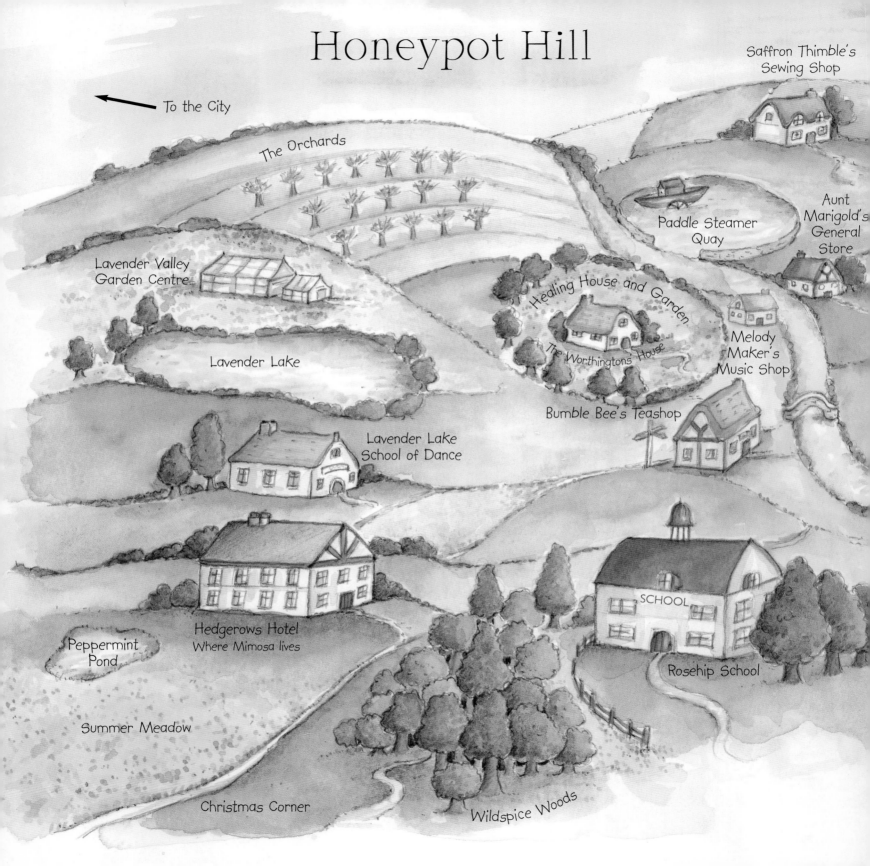

To the City

Saffron Thimble's Sewing Shop

The Orchards

Paddle Steamer Quay

Aunt Marigold's General Store

Lavender Valley Garden Centre

Healing House and Garden

The Worthingtons' House

Melody Maker's Music Shop

Lavender Lake

Bumble Bee's Teashop

Lavender Lake School of Dance

Peppermint Pond

Hedgerows Hotel
Where Mimosa lives

SCHOOL

Rosehip School

Summer Meadow

Christmas Corner

Wildspice Woods

Honeysuckle Cottage
Poppy's House

Forget-Me-Not Cottage
Grandpa's House and Office

Poppy Field

N
W   E
S

Honeypot Cottage
Honey and Granny Bumble's House

Blossom
Bakehouse

Cornsilk Castle
and Courtyard

Village Hall

Sage's
Vet Surgery

Post Office

River Swan

Beehive
Beauty Salon

Barley Farm
The Meadowsweets' House

Riverside
Stables

Honeypot Hill
Railway Station

To Camomile Cove
via Periwinkle Lane

Check out Princess Poppy's brilliant website:

www.princesspoppy.com

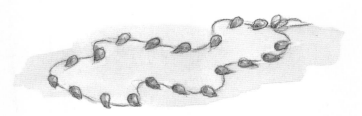

THE PARTY
A PICTURE CORGI BOOK 978 0 552 55926 3

First published in Great Britain by Picture Corgi,
an imprint of Random House Children's Books
A Random House Group Company

This edition published 2009

3 5 7 9 10 8 6 4 2

Text copyright © Janey Louise Jones, 2009
Illustration copyright © Picture Corgi Books, 2009
Illustrations by Veronica Vasylenko
Design by Tracey Cunnell

The right of Janey Louise Jones to be identified as the author of this work has been
asserted in accordance with the Copyright, Designs and Patents Act 1988.

Picture Corgi Books are published by Random House Children's Books,
61–63 Uxbridge Road, London W5 5SA

www.**kidsatrandomhouse**.co.uk
www.princesspoppy.com

Addresses for companies within The Random House Group Limited
can be found at: www.randomhouse.co.uk/offices.htm

THE RANDOM HOUSE GROUP Limited Reg. No. 954009

A CIP catalogue record for this book is available from the British Library.

Printed in China

The Party

Written by Janey Louise Jones

PICTURE CORGI

For jewellery lovers everywhere

The Party *featuring*

Mum

★

Honey

★

Princess Poppy

Granny Bumble

★

Poppy put on her prettiest pink party dress. Today was Honey's birthday and she was having a party in Cornsilk Castle – Poppy was very excited.

Honey was standing at the entrance as her friends arrived.

"Thank you!" she smiled as everyone handed her their prettily wrapped presents.

"Happy birthday, Honey!" said Poppy as she passed her best friend the gift she had made for her.

Honey carefully undid the ribbon, then opened the
paper to reveal a little felt mouse pin cushion.

"It's so cute!" she exclaimed. "I love it!"

When Honey had opened her presents, Granny Bumble
told everyone that it was time for the magic show.

As the children sat down in a large circle, chattering with excitement, the magician rode into the room on a unicycle.

"Hello, boys and girls, I'm Vanishing Victor! Prepare to be amazed!"

He made a fluffy bunny
come out of his hat.

Then a shiny coin magically
appeared from Honey's shoe.

Next he pulled a whole stream of
coloured silk handkerchiefs from his sleeve.

Finally, he made a playing card
disappear then reappear in Poppy's bag!

Everyone clapped and cheered, wishing the show could go on,
but Vanishing Victor was already pedalling towards the door.

   After the magic show, it was time for party games. They played pass
the parcel, musical chairs, sleeping lions and pin the tail on the pony.

Then it was tea time.

"Deeelicious!" said Poppy as she spotted the yummy-looking cheese and cucumber sandwiches, frosted honey buns, chocolate-smothered strawberries and fairy cakes. Everyone tucked in.

Then Granny Bumble brought in a ballerina birthday cake. Honey and all her guests gasped! It was the most amazing cake they had ever seen.

All too soon it was time for the guests to go home.

Honey gave each of her friends two iced fairy cakes in pretty gold boxes and thanked them for coming.

When everyone had left, she and Poppy gathered the presents together. Then they went back to Honey's house to have a proper look at all her birthday things.

There was a cute wooden squirrel, an art and craft set filled with paints, crayons, paper and glue. There was a rag doll, a ballet case, a fairy outfit, pretty clothes, exciting books and a pony-grooming kit.

The final gift was a gorgeous necklace.

"Wow, who gave you that?" asked Poppy,

"Oh, I think it's from Miss Mallow," replied Honey, turning back to her pony-grooming kit.

Just then, the phone rang in the hall. It was Honey's mum and dad calling from America. Honey rushed off excitedly.

Poppy couldn't take her eyes off the beautiful necklace. Each bead was the palest pink and shaped like a rose bud. It would go so well with her dress. Poppy felt as if the necklace was made for her and she wished more than anything that it was hers.

At that moment her thoughts were interrupted by Granny Bumble.

"Poppy," she called through from the kitchen, "you promised your mum you'd be home by now. You'd better get going, sweetheart."

"OK, Granny Bumble. Thank you for the lovely party," replied Poppy as she gathered her things together.

When Poppy got home, she went to her bedroom. She sat on her bed and opened her bag. Inside was the necklace. She fastened it around her neck and admired herself in the mirror.

When Mum called her down for supper, Poppy quickly hid the beads in her pocket, and went to sit at the table. "How was the party?" asked Mum.

"It was really fun," said Poppy. "There was a magician and we played loads of games and Granny Bumble made a delicious birthday tea. Oh, and you should see all Honey's amazing presents! She's so lucky."

As Poppy started to tell Mum all about the presents, the phone rang.

"That was Granny Bumble. One of Honey's presents has gone missing – a string of pink beads. She thought you might have seen them." Mum said.

Poppy went bright red.

"Um, er, no," she replied, and stood up to get herself
a drink. But as she did so, something fell out of her pocket.

"Well, what are those then?" asked Mum.

Poppy burst into tears.

"I'm sorry. I didn't mean to — it's just that Honey had so many presents and I've just borrowed the beads, really," she sobbed.

"Oh, Poppy! Did Honey know that you were borrowing them?" She shook her head.

"Well, it's not borrowing then," said Mum. "They don't belong to you so you shouldn't have taken them."

"I know," admitted Poppy, already feeling very sorry for what she'd done.

"Well, what are you going to do?" asked Mum.

"Um, take the beads back and say sorry?" suggested Poppy.

Mum nodded.

Poppy had butterflies in her tummy as she rang Honey's door bell.

The door opened. Poppy took a deep breath.

"You can't find your pink beads because I took them. I was just borrowing them and I was going to bring them back tomorrow," she explained. "I'm really, really sorry."

"At least you've brought them back now, Poppy," said Granny Bumble. "Come on in."

"Oh, Poppy!" said Honey, hugging her best friend. "I would have let you borrow them, if only you'd asked! You know I don't even like pink!"

"Thank you!" Poppy smiled.

She felt so much better and was glad that Honey wasn't cross with her.

As they left Honey's, Poppy was deep
in thought.

"Mum, am I still a princess?" she asked.

"Yes, you'll always be a princess,
as long as you don't do anything that
naughty ever again!" replied Mum firmly.

When they got home, Mum disappeared upstairs and came back with some beautiful pink beads, even lovelier than Honey's.

"Poppy, these belonged to my mum. I want you to have them because you've been very brave and faced up to what you did today."

"Thank you!" smiled Poppy as Mum put the necklace on her. "They're gorgeous – I promise to always behave like a true princess from now on!"

Princess Poppy